Challenged by
Mental Illness

T0019807

Challenged by Mental Illness

Resting in God's Love

NEELA REDFORD

TATE PUBLISHING
AND ENTERPRISES, LLC

Challenged by Mental Illness
Copyright © 2014 by Neela Redford. All rights reserved.

No part of this publication may be reproduced, stored in a retrieval system or transmitted in any way by any means, electronic, mechanical, photocopy, recording or otherwise without the prior permission of the author except as provided by USA copyright law.

Scripture quotations marked (NIV) are taken from the *Holy Bible, New International Version* ®, Copyright © 1973, 1978, 1984 by International Bible Society. Used by permission of Zondervan Publishing House. All rights reserved.

Scripture quotations marked (KJV) are taken from the Holy Bible, King James Version, Cambridge, 1769. Used by permission. All rights reserved.

The opinions expressed by the author are not necessarily those of Tate Publishing, LLC.

Published by Tate Publishing & Enterprises, LLC
127 E. Trade Center Terrace | Mustang, Oklahoma 73064 USA
1.888.361.9473 | www.tatepublishing.com

Tate Publishing is committed to excellence in the publishing industry. The company reflects the philosophy established by the founders, based on Psalm 68:11,
"The Lord gave the word and great was the company of those who published it."

Book design copyright © 2012 by Tate Publishing, LLC. All rights reserved.
Cover design by Lauro Talibong
Interior design by Ronnel Luspoc

Published in the United States of America

ISBN: 978-1-62295-003-4
1. Biography & Autobiography / Personal Memoirs
2. Self-Help / Depression
14.10.23

Dedication

This book is dedicated to my mother, who always believed in me and always had her million-dollar smile for me.

Contents

Acknowledgments

I wish to acknowledge the following people for walking with me on my journey: Van, Joel, and Trilby, my siblings; Amber and Aaron, my niece and nephew; Cheryl Brown, my dearest friend who encouraged me to write this book; Emmie and Denise for their support and friendship; Dr. Karen Ballou; Dr. Nancy Alford; and First Christian Church.

Trouble and God's Mercy

Does God still perform miracles today? My answer is a resounding yes! I know there may be many people in the world who would scoff at my answer, but I hope I can share my testimony with you and help you believe if you don't already. God is real, his love is real, and he cares about you. If you are mentally ill, I am here to share my hope, and if you are a loved one of a mentally ill person, I want you to read on, because this is for you, too.

My name is Neela Redford. I am a forty-five year old woman who has suffered from mental illness most of my life. The beginning of my illness is a little vague because it started so early. I was a victim of sexual abuse from an early age, which started the depression, the confusion, the lack of identity, the low self-worth, and even self-loathing. As a child, I had no control over my life, so I began to suffer from encopresis, a condition that stems from abuse. It means that I withhold bowel movements and refuse to go until it is absolutely necessary. I was already potty trained, so this was highly irregular behavior. One of my earliest memories is being just tall enough to look out the window and going in my pants. My family was perplexed, I remember, but they did not know what it was or what to do about it. This continued until I was about five years old.

I never felt safe as a young child. I remember when I was five I woke up crying one morning. It was about a year before I started school, and I was fearful at the thought of it. My parents reassured me, but once I started school, I cried every day that first year. I didn't trust anyone and felt that the world was too scary a place. My mother was so sweet; on the last day of first grade she bought me a dollhouse to reward me for enduring the whole school year. I was aware we didn't have much money, so that made it even more special.

The depression continued throughout my school years. Some years I hardly went to school at all. No one seemed to think this was strange enough to ask any questions. It was the 1970s, and I don't think teachers were looking for signs of abuse. My agony continued, because I wasn't even sure what was wrong with me. I didn't put the pieces together until years later.

All of my childhood was not horrible, however. God blessed me with much freedom in the summers of my childhood. I didn't have the added stress of school, and I basically lived outdoors from sunrise to sunset. I had a few friends, and we had many adventures together. God was there all along. He did give me hope in those summers in particular. My friends and I rode bikes all over town, we built houses out of refrigerator boxes, and we went to the movies and library a lot. I thank God for those breaks. They saved my childhood, and they saved my life.

I soon became a teenager, and as is true for so many, those years were stressful and awkward. I was painfully shy, and I think some people at school mistook this for being snobbish. All I could do was focus on my studies and make good grades. Most of my teachers knew I was a serious student, and I gained some self-confidence from doing well and earning the respect of my teachers. God turned a stressful thing like school into a place where I could excel, and this was also a lifesaver.

Things began to get better in high school. I had gained some confidence and began to come out of my shell a little. It was challenging, but I graduated with honors. It was especially challenging because my dad almost died in my senior year. He had apparently been suffering from a stomach ulcer for quite some time. I was at home with him when he started hemorrhaging. I just didn't know what to do. I felt he was going to die. A week later he was rushed to the hospital, and God saved his life. My dad had to quit work in 1979 due to a layoff and the onset of arthritis. The ulcer was his first brush with death. It was a scary experience, and it triggered a bout with depression for me. Thankfully, it didn't last long.

So high school ended, and for the first time in my life I was faced with having to think about my future. What would my future hold?

Roadblocks and a Change in Direction

My French teacher in high school had taken a great interest in my future. Mademoiselle Johnson insisted I meet with the guidance counselor to plan which college I would like to attend. God was good to me by giving me a willing helper to encourage me to even go to college. I didn't know about financial aid at that time, so I had not planned for college. Everything worked out well. I chose a college nearby so that I wouldn't be far from Dad, who had been so sick. I decided I would study accounting since I had enjoyed it in high school. I had a pleasant summer preparing for college. I was actually looking forward to it.

The fall came, and I got settled in the dorm pretty quickly. My roommate was a friend from high school, so that made the adjustments much easier. In October I went with my family to a church festival, and when we were leaving, we were in a car accident. I received the worst of the injuries. I had a severe whiplash and had to wear a neck brace for three months. I stayed in school, but it was difficult trying to concentrate in such pain. In addition, I was finding that I really didn't enjoy accounting as much as I had in high school. I did not try to get a job in accounting. I didn't know what to do with my life. This internal conflict, the pain from the accident, and my dad being diagnosed with congestive heart failure all sent me down the familiar path of depression. I quit school after being there a year and a half.

It felt as though I wouldn't bounce back from this. Part of this feeling was a lack of experience in life. I thought it was the end of the world. I felt like a complete failure. This depression stayed with me for about a year. Then when I received a settlement from the car accident, I paid for a correspondence course in writing for children. I worked diligently on it and finished the course in a year. I had never done much creative writing, and it was what I needed to give me hope that I might have a future doing something I love. I never wrote a children's book, but whenever I got really low, I would think of writing, and my spirits would be lifted.

My father's health got progressively worse. In December 1992, he left home for the hospital for the last time. I had been going to the local community college studying graphic design. On February 8, 1993, he passed away. My brother picked me up from school that morning and gave me the news. I was not shocked, because I had actually said good-bye to him the night before, even though he was not coherent. Still, the grief was heavy. My dad had taught me a lot about life and a lot about everything he knew in general. He was a genius in many ways, and I missed him terribly.

This grief triggered something inside me. All the years of pain I had suffered as a child began to weigh heavily upon me. I couldn't finish the graphic design program due to a financial issue and the depression. I decided to seek professional help.

Seeking Help

I made an appointment with a therapist at the local county mental health center for August 20, 1993. She was very caring and did her best to address the depression. However, on September 26, 1993, I told her I could not handle things anymore. I was not suicidal. However, I was afraid the depression was going to kill me inside.

She immediately got me in to see Dr. Karen Ballou. Dr. Ballou gently asked me if I would be willing to be admitted to the hospital to try some medication. I agreed, because I felt this was the only way I would feel better.

I was uneasy, because I didn't know what to expect from the hospital. I was tempted to stay in bed and pull the covers over my head. The staff was kind, and they kept me busy with group meetings and leisure activities. I was very depressed yet eager to be involved so I could get better. I met some wonderful people in those staff members, and I am grateful to this day for people who are willing to do that kind of work.

My first hospital stay was about five weeks long. I came out armed with new information on coping skills, but I still was not much better. I also came out with a twelve thousand dollar hospital bill that I didn't know how I was going to pay. God worked that out. In six months I was on disability, and my insurance went retroactive to pay the hospital bill. God is so good!

The first few years of my treatment I was in the hospital more than I was out of it. My depression worsened, and Dr. Ballou suggested I have ECT. ECT is electroconvulsive therapy, and I had fifteen of them—nine in 1994 and six in 1997. In ECT I was put under anesthesia. They put two electrodes on my head and sent a small current through my brain. It stimulated brain chemicals and brain activity. I had six ECT treatments again in December 2011and January 2012 because the medication alone wasn't working. I am doing much better.

As I have said, depression has been with me all of my life. However, starting in 1995, I had symptoms of schizoaffective disorder, which is schizophrenia and bipolar disorder, in my case. I started hearing voices and seeing things that were not there. I was not only suffering from depression, but I was having manic episodes. When I was manic, I would have grandiose thoughts and stay on the computer all night long searching randomly for whatever popped into my head. I once thought I would be a great asset to the FBI. Thankfully, I didn't pursue that idea.

I felt like an alien in my own skin. I could not sleep (not since age twelve really), and everything usually seemed like it was spinning out of control. I found it hard to be coherent, and a positive thought hardly ever entered my thinking. During this whole ordeal, I even found it nearly impossible to pray. All I could do was cry out for God to help me. But the worst was not over yet.

Suicide and God's Saving Grace

There were many years when I thought I would not make it. Much of the time I didn't want to make it. In 1995, I attempted suicide for the first time. I took a bottle of anti-anxiety pills. Then I told my mom what I had done. My brother rushed me to the hospital, and I passed out before they pumped my stomach. This was a blessing, because I have heard horror stories about people having to be conscious while their stomachs were pumped. At any rate God brought me through it.

My second suicide attempt was more desperate and bold. On the night of January 15, 2001, I got some rope, made an excuse to my family for going outside, and I started walking. I walked quickly; I couldn't run because my legs felt like rubber. I found a tree on the railroad bank and tried to hang myself. But once again, God stepped in.

I was too weak and out of breath to tie the rope. I sat on the ground and felt totally numb. I felt no emotions. I was actually thinking that an angel might appear because I felt dead. After a while, I made it back home, too weak to speak. My brother called Dr. Ballou, and she got me admitted to the hospital. I have been in the hospital over thirty times in eighteen years. When I think of what everybody went through around me, I am amazed that anyone stood by me, but they did. I am especially grateful for the dedication of Dr. Ballou. She is a humble woman of God and a prayer warrior. I am sure she has interceded for me in prayer a countless number of times. I thank God for her every day. Her sweet, gentle manner kept me going through the hardest times of my life.

My mother also prayed for me, and she always wanted to make sure I was okay. She passed away on October 5, 2011, after a long illness. She was a faith-filled woman of God who never gave up. She was a wonderful example for me, and I treasure the times I had with her in those last months. She taught me a lot by the way she lived.

Moving Forward and Believing in Miracles

In an attempt to be on my own and not be a burden to my family, I stayed in two different rest homes. The first one was in 2000, and I went there straight from the hospital. The second one was in 2001 after leaving the hospital and waiting for an apartment to become available. I could not make myself content to be there, so I moved back home and stayed there five years.

I was able to get an associate's degree in electronics during that time, which was one of my happiest achievements. It was especially meaningful, because during that time my mom had a heart attack while in the car with me and basically died as I rushed her to the hospital. They had to use the defibrillator three times to bring her back. God was in the midst of this every step of the way, because the timing of all of the events was perfect. She was on life support for ten days before she could breathe on her own. When she was able to speak, she told of us an incredible miracle.

She said she went to heaven and there were lots of people she knew standing there. She said it was a beautiful city, and she looked and saw Jesus standing on a hill in the middle of the city. He said to her, "Well done!"

This story amazed us, and she shared it with nurses in the hospital, who were also amazed. I tell this story even today, because it is wonderfully encouraging and inspiring.

A Turning Point

The year 2010 was perhaps my most difficult year. I began to have delusions that Satan was attacking me in bed at night and was throwing me around the room. This happened for three nights in a row. The next night I stayed up all night praying, asking God to remove Satan, because he has no place in my home. It seemed so real. It was especially frightening because I lived alone.

I told my doctor, and she convinced me it was a delusion. I was hospitalized three times due to the delusions, and the depression was really bad. I felt so alone, more than I ever had. The medication wasn't really working very well, but I went home after Christmas that year determined that things were going to have to be different.

The year 2011 was a better year, but I suffered a bout of depression after my mom passed away in October. God has not left me in despair; he encourages me with his great love and compassion and has shown me what a wonderful parent he is now that both my parents are in heaven. He has given me a wonderful church family, and they pray for me. It is such a beautiful blessing. I am finally learning to trust God, and I know that everything I have been through is part of his plan to mold and shape me into a new creation.

Whatever you go through, lean on God. Rest in him, knowing that you are safe in his arms. He loves you unconditionally—there is nothing you can do to make him love you any less than he does now.

Reflections

My relationship with God has grown since he revealed himself to me when I was a child. My parents started teaching me about God when I was three, and I began to see him as my father. When I was old enough to read, I read Bible stories then the Bible itself. I began to learn about the sacrifice God made when Jesus came to earth. At first I didn't understand why Jesus had to die for us, but when I learned why he did it, I was astounded to realize the gift of grace. Jesus took all our sins upon him at the cross, and now we can live with God for eternity. As my mom's miracle underscores, heaven is a reality. Thanks and praise belong to Jesus for this precious gift!

Several scriptures that I enjoy reading gave me great encouragement.

- God is love. "He that loveth not knoweth not God; for God is love" (1 John 4:8). We worship a God who *is* love. If we have God in us, we can love God and others more perfectly. Read 1 Corinthians 13 in its entirety, because the apostle Paul describes love in detail. Without love, we are nothing.

- God makes all things possible. "But Jesus beheld them, and said unto them, 'With men this is impossible, but with God all things are possible'" (Matthew 19:26). Jesus was speaking of salvation in this text. Mark 10:27 states the same message. Luke states it this way: "And he said, 'The things which are impossible with men are possible with God'" (Luke 18:27). When I look back at my journey, I realize I didn't always believe this with my whole heart. But his Word is true; God cannot lie.

- God heals. "But he was wounded for our transgressions, he was bruised for our iniquities: the chastisement of our peace was upon him: and with his stripes we are healed" (Isaiah 53:5). This is a prophecy concerning Jesus's crucifixion for our salvation. His saving work included healing our illnesses. We have to claim it by faith. The Lord *is* willing and *is* able to heal, and it is our task to believe.

- God has plans for you. "For I know the thoughts that I think toward you, saith the Lord, thoughts of peace, and not of evil, to give you an unexpected end" (Jeremiah 29:11, KJV). I also like the New International Version's translation of this scripture: "For I know the plans I have for you, declares the Lord, plans to prosper you and not to harm you, plans to give you a hope and a future" (Jeremiah

29:11, NIV). This was written to the Israelites who were exiles in Babylon. It can be applied to us today. We are subject to "exile" on this earth when we suffer, but God has a plan and a purpose for each one of us.

- God will never leave you. There are several scriptures that address this in various situations in the Bible. "(For the Lord thy God is a merciful God): He will not forsake thee, neither destroy thee, nor forget the covenant of thy fathers which he sware unto them" (Deuteronomy 4:31). He was speaking of the Israelites, but it can be applied to us, too. In Deuteronomy 31, Moses told Israel twice in verses six and eight that God would not fail them or forsake them, and that they should not be afraid. This was just before they entered the Promised Land. God is with us in all seasons of our lives, and he has promised to never leave us.

- God desires to bless you. "He will bless them that fear the Lord, both small and great. The Lord shall increase you more, you and your children. Ye are blessed of the Lord which made heaven and earth" (Psalms 115:13-15). God is the greatest giver of all!

- God is our hope. "For thou art my hope, O Lord God: thou art my trust from my youth" (Psalms 71:5). We can have hope in this life and a hope in

God for an eternity of peace and joy. Trust in God, and let him be your hope.

- God encourages. "These things I have spoken unto you, that in me ye might have peace. In the world ye shall have tribulation: but be of good cheer: I have overcome the world" (John 16:33). I have turned to this scripture time after time when I needed encouragement. Jesus is saying that he has the victory over our tribulation!

- God strengthens. "I can do all things through Christ which strengtheneth me" (Philippians 4:13). Jesus strengthened me so that I could face all the trials in my life.

- God will gather you under his wings. "Keep me as the apple of thy eye, hide me under thy wings" (Psalms 17:8). God is like a mother hen who gathers her chicks under her wings to protect them and comfort them.

- God saves. "For God so loved the world, that he gave his only begotten son, that whosoever believeth in him, should not perish, but have everlasting life" (John 3:16). God wants everyone to be with him forever!

- God forgives. "For thou, Lord, art good, and ready to forgive: and plenteous in mercy unto all them that call upon thee" (Psalms 86:5). All of us have sinned, and thanks be to God who is ready to forgive!

- God rebukes the enemy. "And Jesus answered and said unto him, 'Get thee behind me, Satan: for it is written, Thou shalt worship the Lord thy God, and him only shalt thou serve'" (Luke 4:8). Jesus rebuked Satan, and he used the Word to do it. Many times I have asked Jesus to help me rebuke Satan, because I knew the enemy was trying his best to destroy me through my illness.

- God gives you gifts. Read the entire chapter of 1 Corinthians 12, because it describes the spiritual gifts God gives us to become more like him and to spread the good news of Jesus's victory over sin and death in our lives.

- God is our fortress. "The Lord is my rock, and my fortress, and my deliverer: my God, my strength in whom I will trust: my buckler, and the horn of my salvation, and my high tower" (Psalms 18:2). We are in a spiritual battle, and we need God to protect and deliver us.

- God reveals himself. "He revealeth the deep and secret things; he knoweth what is in the darkness, and the light dwelleth with him" (Daniel 2:22). For those who seek him, God reveals knowledge.

- The Holy Spirit brings to your remembrance the Word of God. "But the Comforter, which is the Holy Ghost, whom the Father will send in my name, he shall teach you all things, and bring all things to your remembrance, whatsoever I have said unto you" (John 14:26). When we study God's Word, the Holy Spirit seals it in our hearts and helps us to remember it.

- The Holy Spirit won't let you give up on God. The Holy Spirit kept me from going through with the suicide attempts. The Comforter goes with us, and he has definitely walked with me throughout my whole ordeal.

- Jesus is our high priest who intercedes for us. "Wherefore he is able also to save them to the uttermost that come unto God by him, seeing he ever liveth to make intercession for them. For such an high priest became us, who is holy, harmless, undefiled, separate from sinners, and made higher than the heavens" (Hebrews 7:25-26). Jesus speaks to the Father on our behalf!

- Jesus prepares a place for us. "In my Father's house are many mansions: if it were not so, I would have told you. I go to prepare a place for you. And if I go and prepare a place for you, I will come again, and receive you unto myself: that where I am, there ye may be also" (John 14:2-3). At times, I could not bear to think about going on in this life. I would think of these verses, and they would lift my spirits. Eternal life with God in a heavenly mansion! What an awesome truth!

- Jesus is your friend. "Ye are my friends, if ye do whatsoever I command you. Henceforth, I call you not servants: for the servant knoweth not what his lord doeth: but I have called you friends: for all things that I have heard of my Father I have made known unto you" (John 15:14-15). Friends spend time together and get to know each other. I enjoy my time with Jesus.

- God's mercy endures forever. "O give thanks unto the Lord: for he is good: for his mercy endureth for ever" (1 Chronicles 16:34). His tender mercy keeps me going.

- We can enter into the Father's presence, the Holy of Holies, because of Jesus. "And, behold, the veil of the temple was rent in twain from the top to the bottom: and the earth did quake, and the rocks rent..." (Matthew 27:51). When Jesus died on the cross, the veil in the temple split in two, and the most holy Father became available to us, because our sins no longer separated us from him. We can now have a direct relationship with the Father.

- Jesus bears our burdens. My favorite scripture at my worst times was this: "Come unto me, all ye that labour and are heavy laden, and I will give you rest. Take my yoke upon you, and learn of me: for I am meek and lowly in heart: and ye shall find rest unto your souls. For my yoke is easy, and my burden is light" (Matthew 11:28-30). When yoked with Jesus, he shoulders our burdens for us. This scripture has been a tremendous blessing for me.

- God gives us a sound mind. "For God hath not given us the spirit of fear: but of power, and of love, and of a sound mind" (2 Timothy 1:7). I have relied on this verse throughout my life. Go to God with this verse in prayer, and ask for the spirit of a sound mind.

- God is patient. "Now the God of patience and consolation grant you to be likeminded one toward another according to Christ Jesus" (Romans 15:5). God is patient and calls us to be patient. I hate to admit that I was not always patient with God or others when I was suffering. However, it is through suffering that God produces patience in us.

- We worship God because he is worthy. "Thou art worthy, O Lord, to receive glory and honour and power: for thou hast created all things, and for thy pleasure they are and were created" (Revelation 4:11). We worship God whether we are sick or healed because we are created by him. God loves us so much. How else should we respond to him?

Scripture is the living Word of God. God speaks to us powerfully through Scripture, and if we are Christians suffering with mental illness, we need to read God's Word every day. Accompanied by praying for God to protect our minds, reading his Word empowers us to fight the battle of our minds. Satan, our enemy, seeks to destroy us and uses our weaknesses to do it. Ultimately, Jesus Christ won the victory over Satan. But we still need to be careful about the satanic influence in this world around us. Cling to God, and ask him to keep you in perfect peace. God is more than willing to heal us. We must exercise faith and trust in God.

Although I am not healed, I eagerly await the day God heals me. My faith is not yet perfected, and I have a lot to overcome, but I encourage you to wait patiently on God. He loves us more than our minds can begin to imagine.

Many books have been written about who God is and what he does. Mine is only based on my personal experience with God, but it is my prayer that you will be blessed by the testimony God has given me. You may be asking yourself, "What now?" Well, if you have not accepted Jesus Christ as your Lord and Savior, I think that would be a good next step. Jesus will send you the Comforter, and he will teach you and lead you into the wonders of God. Pray this prayer:

> *Lord Jesus, I know you love me. Please be my Lord and Savior. I repent of my sins and ask for you to create in me a pure heart. I make you the ruler of my life and ask that you save me so that I may spend eternity with you. Please heal my mind. Turn the disorder into order, oh, God. Help my thoughts to be clear, and heal my broken heart. Thank you, Jesus! Hallelujah!*

Now let your journey to eternity begin!